Holidays

THE

Best Easter Eggs EVER!

For Shannon McKeon
—J.S.

SCHOLASTIC, CARTWHEEL BOOKS, and associated logos are trademarks and/or registered trademarks of Scholastic Inc. No part of this publication may be reproduced, or stored in a retrieval system, or transmitted in any form or by any means, electronic, mechanical, photocopying, recording, or otherwise, without written permission of the publisher. For information regarding permission, write to Scholastic Inc., Attention: Permissions Department, 557 Broadway, New York, NY 10012.

ISBN 0-439-44321-0

Library of Congress Cataloging-in-Publication Data available

10 9 8 7 6 5 4 3 2 1   03 04 05 06 07

Printed in the U.S.A.   24
First printing, February 2003

Holidays

THE Best Easter Eggs EVER!

by
Jerry Smath

Cartwheel
B·O·O·K·S ®

SCHOLASTIC INC.

New York   Toronto   London   Auckland   Sydney   Mexico City
New Delhi   Hong Kong   Buenos Aires

Springtime had finally come and
Easter was almost here.

This was a busy time for Easter Bunny,
who painted all the Easter eggs himself.

Each of Easter Bunny's little helpers had a special job to do, too.

Willa Bunny was in charge of weaving the Easter baskets.

Jellybean Bunny filled them with marshmallow chicks, chocolate, and jelly beans.

And Bella Bunny tied a beautiful bow to the handle of each basket.

"I like your polka-dot eggs," she said to Easter Bunny.

"Thank you," said Easter Bunny, "but I need a new design for my eggs this year. I see polka dots even when I'm not painting them."

"Can we help you?" asked his helpers.

Easter Bunny thought a while, then said, "Maybe you can!"

Easter Bunny handed each of them an unpainted egg and a paint box with brushes.

"Let's have an Easter Egg Painting Contest!" he said. "Whoever paints the best Easter egg wins. And the winner can paint their design on all the Easter eggs this year."

The three little bunnies cheered! Then each one went in a different direction, hoping to find something pretty to paint.

"Be back in time for dinner," called Easter Bunny. "We're having carrot stew tonight."

Willa Bunny loved the seashore—so that's where she went.

While curious seagulls looked on, she scanned
the beach for something interesting to paint.

It didn't take long. Not far away stood a tall
lighthouse with bold red stripes.

Willa took out her widest brush and painted
those same red stripes on her egg.

Because he loved spring colors, Jellybean Bunny's search took him to the country.

Spring flowers everywhere showed off their beautiful colors, as if to say, "Paint me!"

So that is just what Jellybean Bunny did. Using his prettiest colors, he painted flowers on his egg.

Bella Bunny walked and walked but didn't see anything she wanted to paint.

Then looking up, she saw fluffy white clouds floating across the blue sky. One looked like a bird. Another looked like a carrot. One cloud even looked like Easter Bunny!

Bella thought the clouds would be fun to paint on her egg. But when she stopped to paint them, the wind blew the clouds further away, over the woods. Bella kept running after them.

Deeper and deeper into the woods she ran.
Suddenly, the sky grew dark and the clouds
disappeared. Bella Bunny found herself tired and
alone—without ever having painted her egg.

She was trying to find her way out of the dark
woods when the moon suddenly appeared.

Then, one by one, stars began to fill the night sky.

Suddenly, Bella knew what her Easter egg design would be! She took out her brush and, by the light of the moon, started painting her egg with golden stars.

Easter Bunny was in the kitchen cooking his stew when Willa and Jellybean returned.

"Where is Bella?" he asked.

"On our way here we saw her running into the woods," said his helpers.

Easter Bunny was worried. "We must go and look for her right away!" he said.

Using flashlights to light their way, Easter Bunny,
Willa, and Jellybean went into the dark woods.
"Bella...Bella...Bella!" they called as they searched.

Finally they found her—she was
sound asleep in her wheelbarrow.
Easter Bunny gently picked up his little
sleeping helper. Then Jellybean led
the way out of the woods.

Once at home, all three bunnies were put to bed.
"It's been a busy day for all of you," said Easter
Bunny. "Tomorrow, after a good night's rest, I'll look
at the eggs you've painted."

WILLA

JELLYBEAN

When morning came, Willa Bunny was the first
to hop out of bed.

"Wake up, everyone!" she called. "Today Easter
Bunny picks one of our designs for his Easter eggs!"

"Here he comes now," Bella said sleepily.

The bunnies proudly held up their eggs. Easter Bunny looked at each one very carefully.

"I've never seen such bold red stripes," he said to Willa.

"And look at those pretty flowers," he said to Jellybean.

"Your stars shine brighter than the real ones," he said to Bella.

"You **all** win the contest!" said Easter Bunny.
"I want all of your designs on my Easter eggs this year."
Then he hung a bright gold medal on each of
their creations.

The three bunnies were overjoyed. They started to paint the Easter eggs right away.

Willa Bunny painted her bold red stripes.
Jellybean Bunny painted his pretty flowers.
And Bella Bunny painted her shiny gold stars.

Easter Bunny smiled as he watched his little helpers at work.

"This year's Easter eggs will be the best Easter eggs ever!" he said.